Airshow!

Written by
Mark A. Hewitt

Illustrated by
Nikki Mate

Daddy asked,
"Want to go to an airshow?"
"What's an airshow?"

Brother said, "They have airplanes!"
Sister said, "They have jets!"
Daddy said, "Maybe we'll see helicopters. It's an aircraft that has wings that spin on top."

Brother said, "Airplanes are loud!"
Sister said, "Jets are fast!"
Daddy said, "Helicopters go slow, can stop and hover. They can go up and down."
"What's a hoover?"
"Hover," said Mommy. She lifted her hand over the table and said, "Hover is suspended over a place or object."

I didn't understand. When I try to make my spoon hover, it would fall on the floor.

Brother said, "Airplanes fly low!"
Sister said, "Jets fly high!"
Daddy said, "Helicopters can fly backwards."
I didn't understand how helicopters could go backwards. I would fall down. They must have eyes on the back of its head.

Brother said, "Airplanes are small!"

Sister said, "Jets are big!"

Daddy said, "Helicopters can pick up things."

"What kinds of things?"

"People, puppies, and pickups," said Mommy.

I didn't understand. I think a helicopter is a monster.
I was afraid to go to the airshow.

Brother was excited! He grabbed his hat.
Sister was excited! She took her sunglasses.
Daddy was excited! He picked up the car keys.
Mommy was excited! She took her purse.

We drove to a place called, "Airport."
Daddy said, "Airshows are at airports."
Brother said, "Airports are for small airplanes!"
Sister said, "Airports are for big jets!"

Daddy pointed. "See! Helicopter.
Helicopters are different.
This one is small. It is slow.
It is noisy. It flies low."

"Look at all of the airplanes and jets and the helicopter at the airshow," said Mommy.
I did not understand these things, big and small and different. I wanted to get closer to see better.

We walked and walked and walked until I saw something big and something small and something strange.

Brother pointed. He said, "See! Airplane! It is small. It is loud. It flies low."
Sister pointed. She said, "See! Jet! Jets are big. It is fast. It flies high."

"We can talk to the pilots. Would you like to talk to the pilots?" asked Mommy.
I nodded and said, "Yes! Please."

Brother took my hand. We walked and stopped at a small airplane. Brother talked to the pilot. The airplane pilot talked about his airplane. "It is loud. It has a propeller and a motor. It has wings and a tail and tires and wheels."

Sister took my hand. We walked and stopped at a big jet. Sister talked to the pilot. The jet pilot talked about his jet. "It is fast. It flies high. It has an engine and wings and a tail and tires and wheels."

Mommy took my hand.
We walked and stopped at the helicopter.
Then the helicopter pilot asked me
if I wanted to sit in the pilot seat.
"Yes, please!"
Not Brother. Not Sister. Not Daddy or Mommy.

The pilot showed me “controls” and boxes and instruments and lights.
She put a helmet on my head.
Brother was sad. Sister laughed.
Daddy smiled. Mommy took my picture.

The helicopter pilot said
the airshow was about to start.
I was so excited!

The airplanes rumbled. They were loud.
There were many others.
Brother said, "That is a loop the loop."
I was scared when smoke came out of the airplane.
I was not scared when smoke came out of the jet.

Then it was the helicopter's turn. My friend the helicopter pilot waved at me. Then the helicopter took off. It lifted up and stopped like a hummingbird. Daddy said, "See! The helicopter is in a hover. Off the ground. Not moving."

I was so excited. Hover! Hummingbirds and bees can hover like a helicopter!
Daddy said, "See! The helicopter does not go fast."
I was very excited.
Daddy said, "See! The helicopter goes up and it goes down! It goes backwards. It goes sideways. It goes forward. Off of the ground. Wasn't that fun?"
I clapped so hard my hands hurt! I was so very excited.

Brother wanted to talk to the airplane pilot.

Sister wanted to talk to the jet pilot.

I wanted to talk to the helicopter pilot. I asked her, "How do you become a pilot?"

The helicopter pilot took her helmet off and said, "When I was a little girl, my Mommy and Daddy took me to an airshow. I saw many airplanes and lots of jets. The helicopter pilot let me sit in his seat. He let me wear his helmet."

"Like me?"
"Yes, just like you did."

"I read airplane books. I drew airplanes and jets and helicopters. I collected pictures of all kinds of aircraft. I knew I wanted to be a pilot. I worked hard in school. I minded my Mommy and Daddy. And I saved my money for flying lessons."

"When you get a little bit bigger, you will be so excited to sit in the seat. Wear a helmet. Buckle in. Start the engine. Take off. Go fast. Go high. Then you have to land. You will be so excited, you will want to do it again and again and again."
She shook my hand and said, "Good luck."
I waved goodbye. I wasn't sad.
Daddy said there is more to see at the airshow.

Brother got a picture of an airplane at the airshow.
Sister got a picture of a jet at the airshow.
Daddy bought me an airshow hat.
I got a picture of the helicopter.
The helicopter pilot signed the picture.
Mommy took my picture in front of airshow airplanes and jets, and with the helicopter pilot.

The airshow was over. Then I was sad.
It was a long walk to our car. We walked and walked and walked.
Brother was tired and fell asleep.
I think the airplane was his favorite.
Sister was sunburned and rubbed lotion on her arms.
I think the jet was her favorite.
Daddy was happy to see airplanes and jets and helicopters.
I think the helicopter was his favorite.
Mommy asked, "Did you have fun at the airshow?"
I nodded and smiled at her.
I asked Daddy, "Can we go to the airshow next year?"
Mommy and Daddy looked at each other and smiled.

I smiled too.

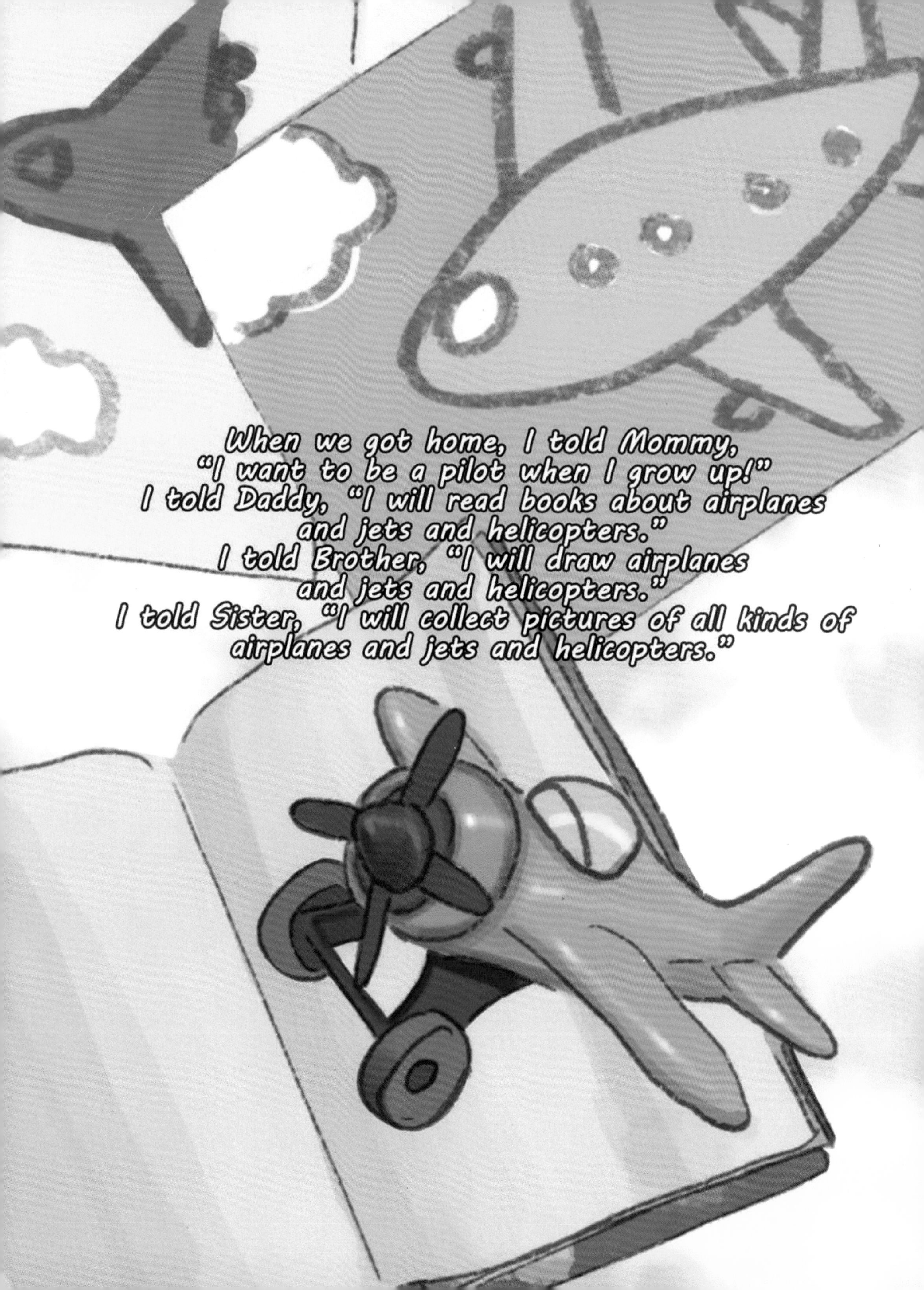

When we got home, I told Mommy,
"I want to be a pilot when I grow up!"
I told Daddy, "I will read books about airplanes
and jets and helicopters."
I told Brother, "I will draw airplanes
and jets and helicopters."
I told Sister, "I will collect pictures of all kinds of
airplanes and jets and helicopters."

I want to be a pilot and go to airshows!
I hope Mommy and Daddy take Brother,
Sister, and me to more airshows
Airshows are so much fun.
Can we go tomorrow?

The aircraft of AIRSHOW!

The Author

Mark A. Hewitt is a former Marine Corps F-4 Phantom pilot and the author of several thrillers.

The Illustrator

Nikki Mate is an Air Force B-1B Pilot. When not flying in airshows herself or drawing, she also likes ponies and puppies and pancakes!

The final approval for this literary material is granted by the author.

First printing

ISBN: 978-1-61296-936-7
PUBLISHED BY BLACK ROSE WRITING
www.blackrosewriting.com

Printed in the United States of America
Airshow! is printed in MV Bovi

BLACK ROSE writing™

CPSIA information can be obtained at www.ICGtesting.com
Printed in the USA
BVIW12n1023250418
PP8635200001B/1